THE
Marvelous Market
ON
MERMAID

BY LAURA KRAUSS MELMED

ILLUSTRATED BY MARYANN KOVALSKI

LOTHROP, LEE & SHEPARD BOOKS • NEW YORK

Lothrop, Lee & Shepard Books,
a division of William Morrow & Company, Inc., 1350 Avenue of the Americas,
New York, New York 10019.
Printed in Hong Kong.
First Edition   1 2 3 4 5 6 7 8 9 10
Library of Congress Cataloging in Publication Data
Melmed, Laura. The Marvelous Market on Mermaid / by Laura Krauss Melmed;
illustrated by Maryann Kovalski.
          p.   cm.
Summary: Describes Gran's store and the goings-on there in
humorous, cumulative fashion.
ISBN 0-688-13053-4. — ISBN 0-688-13054-2 (lib. bdg.)
[1. Grandmothers—Fiction. 2. Stores, Retail—Fiction.
3. Stories in rhyme.] I. Kovalski, Maryann, ill. II. Title.
PZ8.3.M55155Mar 1996 [E]—dc20 93-32621 CIP AC

This is the door on Grandma's store,

the Marvelous Market on Mermaid.

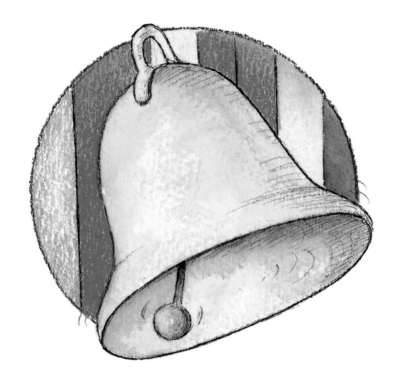

This is the bell that ting-a-lings
when someone opens up the door—
the sky blue door on Grandma's store,
the Marvelous Market on Mermaid.

Through is the yellow bird who sings
each time the doorbell ting-a-lings
when someone opens up the door—
the sky blue door on Grandma's store,
the Marvelous Market on Mermaid.

This is the fat round cheese behind
the glass-front counter you will find
beside the yellow bird who sings
each time the doorbell ting-a-lings
when someone opens up the door—
the sky blue door on Grandma's store,
the Marvelous Market on Mermaid.

This is the man in the tattered hat
who's looking through the window at
the fat round cheese that sits behind
the glass-front counter you will find
beside the yellow bird who sings
each time the doorbell ting-a-lings
when someone opens up the door—
the sky blue door on Grandma's store,
the Marvelous Market on Mermaid.

These are the crumbs that flutter down
when Grandma cuts the loaf so brown
to give a big slice to the man,
a slice she's spread with butter and
a piece of cheese that sat behind
the glass-front counter you will find
beside the yellow bird who sings
each time the doorbell ting-a-lings
when someone opens up the door—
the sky blue door on Grandma's store,
the Marvelous Market on Mermaid.

This is the timid, whiskered mouse
who tiptoes from his hidden house
to eat the crumbs that flutter down
when Grandma cuts the loaf so brown . . .

EEEEEK! The cat goes flashing — s t r e e e a k —
to catch the mouse who scurries — squeeeak —
as crates and cartons crash and clatter,
cookies crumble, bottles shatter.
Grandma gives a little shout,

the cage falls down, the bird flies out,
potatoes pong and apples ping,
there's ketchup over everything —
and as a wobbly shelf goes BAM!
the man says, "Let me help you, ma'am!"

Here's how the man takes up the broom
and sweeps it, swish, across the room.
MEEEOW! The cat sails through the door,
the bird's locked up, her cage secure,
the mouse into his hole has popped,
and I have found the pail and mop.
The man says, "I'll be on my way,"
but Grandma stops him. "Won't you stay?
A strong assistant would be fine
to help me run this store of mine."

"I'd be delighted," says the man,
who tells us that his name is Stan.
Just then the bell goes ting-a-ling,
the yellow bird begins to sing,
and Mrs. Flugle, Mr. Flynn,
and Miss Focaccia all march in.
We sell them pickles, parsnips, pie —
we're quite a team, Gran, Stan, and I!
Says Grandma when the folks have gone,
"Good work! Let's put the kettle on."

And as at last we close the store,
the cat sneaks back inside the door—
the sky blue door on Grandma's store,
the Marvelous Market on Mermaid.